the WITCH and the WISH

Book I - Tales of Obsedea

RYAN DECKARD

Second paperback edition November 2021

Edited by Nicole Alyssa Gabert
Cover art by Xtlinart and Liloupop.art
Maps by Timothy J Gonzales
All inside digital art owned with full rights from Shutterstock

ISBN 979-8-7681-8137-6 (paperback)

Published by Ryan Deckard

Greeting gentle reader,

My name is Mark Timmony, and it is my great honour to have been asked to pen the Foreword of *The Witch and the Wish*, remastered by Ryan Deckard.

I first met Ryan through Instagram in 2018. I was an aspiring author back then, trying to build an audience by posting flash fiction pieces, and Ryan, an accomplished street poet, was working on his own first novel. We got to talking via chat, and to be honest it began with Ryan fanboying over my own prose, and he eventually asked me to read some of his work.

Little did he know I had already read parts of his episodic work on another of his accounts, and I knew he had raw talent. I liked what I read, but there was—as with all of us—room for improvement. At the time, I didn't know how serious Ryan was about his writing; lots of people want to write, and many do spend years practising at it, working on refining their craft. I didn't know where Ryan stood on that scale and how hard he was prepared to work, so when he sent me some of his writing, I sent it back with a response that while I thought it showed promise, I wouldn't be able to read it as he was writing in an omniscient narration and that just wasn't my thing. While once in vogue during the '80s and early '90s, omniscient narration has given way to tight third-person narrative. I cut my teeth on omniscient narration, reading the big names of the '80s and spent a long time moving away from it in my own writing, so much so that these days my internal editor starts getting out the metaphoric red pen when I come across it. But that's just me, which I explained to Ryan regretfully. As it turns out, Ryan also cut his teeth on the big names of the '80s, in forming many of his own stylistic influences.

Rather than be discouraged by my inability to read his work, Ryan threw himself into refining his craft; to bring it into line with a tighter, more character-driven narrative when crafting his words, and that has made all the difference. This novella is not Ryan's first work of long-form fiction; this piece of work was where Ryan mastered and developed his own style and voice as a writer and where he first began to look into the fairy tales and legends as source material to spark his own creative process. Those experiments led to this book that you hold in your hands today. Experimenting with his own gift for poetry, his love of writers like Poe and Stephen King and his keen interest in mythology and the original fairy tales of the Brothers Grimm, Ryan began to write *The Witch and the Wish*.

Ryan's way with words and his gift as a poet shines in every sentence in this brilliantly realised fairy tale of fantasy fiction. Delving into his own worldbuilding, he has pulled from its lore a story much like those of medieval Europe (before they were Disneyfied). He has presented an eerie, spine-tingling, cautionary tale of what happens when children disregard the warnings of their elders and venture into forbidden woods. I have been captivated by Ryan's growth as a storyteller. While economical in parts, Ryan's use of language shines with colour, and he masterfully builds tension as the story progresses, bringing the reader to a shocking ending. But it is skill at depicting young Jacob, the Witch and her companion that really shines and bears the hallmark that makes Ryan Deckard a writer to watch.

I am very proud of Ryan, his growth as a writer, his determination to overcome his own demons, and his persistence in honing his craft. He has worked very hard to refine his first attempts and bring to the world this definitive, remastered edition of his debut, *The Witch and the Wish*. I hope you enjoy it as much as I did.

Mark Timmony,
Sydney, Australia 2021

ACKNOWLEDGEMENTS

So many people have played a role in helping me get to where I am today, and I am eternally grateful. If not for your support, I wouldn't be on this journey. When I didn't think I could do it and was struggling with imposter syndrome, you all pushed me and helped me believe I could do this.

First and foremost, I would like to thank the Uddin family. Sam and Kazi, I appreciate you for making me feel at home in Pittsburgh. Sam, I appreciate all of your advice and support. Kazi, you're amazing and you are like a sister to me. Thank you.

Lori Zaremba, thank you for pointing me in the right direction and getting it into my head to pursue this in the first place. Getting on the train to Pittsburgh was the best thing to happen to me.

Twinkle Varshney, you've always been my biggest supporter and fan and without you I would never beat this point. You're my best friend and I couldn't do it without you.

A special thank you to Mark Timmony. I appreciate all of your writing advice and helping me along this journey. You're truly a great friend.

Nicole Alyssa Gabert, I am extremely grateful to you for editing this manuscript and your meticulous attention to detail. I am beyond grateful to you and your efforts.

James Clarke, thank you for taking the time to beta read and give me honest feedback. I'm happy to have you as a friend.

To my artists, @Xtlinart & @Liloupop.art, thank you for the artwork. The art is phenomenal and I'm excited about the projects to come.

XAENTIS
ISLES OF MIR
PORT TIERE
H SEA
HEART POOL
THE ROYAL RANGE
DRUMOR
THE ROYAL FOREST
TARA LAKE
TARA
THE CAPITAL XAENTIS
THE FORBIDDEN WOOD
ILRUN
DALGRIN

PROLOGUE

A long time ago on a faraway world, a small village sat nestled on the edge of a realm known as the Kingdom of Xaentis. The first light of dawn was beginning to penetrate the darkness, causing a sleepy stir within the village as people started to wake. On a small farm just east of the village, a boy slept a dreamless sleep. He neither tossed nor turned as he slumbered; only floated in darkness.

Until a crow screamed outside his window...

ACT I

JACOB WOKE with a jump and looked around the room. All was in order it seemed. A shiver crept up his spine when his feet hit the floor. Blistering wind intruded from the open window, and he slammed it shut with a thunderous crack. He wasted no time, swiftly changing his clothes. He gave his face a quick scrub in the wash basin, bracing himself for Mama's wrath.

"She gives me much too hard a time," he said, and huffed. "I was only teasing her about going into the woods. She should know I wouldn't do as much."

A grin curled at his lips. He could still see the shock on her face when he told her that he'd ventured beyond the edge of the village. "Maybe she shouldn't be so foolish."

"Jacob!" He jumped at the sound of his mother's voice, her tone harsh. The grin he wore tightened into a grimace. "Get your lazy hide out of bed and come eat. I'll feed it to the dogs, don't think I won't. They've been twice as long without a hot meal in their bellies, and they're twice as deserving."

He cursed beneath his breath. If either of his parents caught him speaking this way, last night's supper wouldn't be the only meal he missed. "Sooner or later, they will have to treat me as a man. I'm in my twelfth cycle after all."

He gazed upon himself in the reflecting glass and scrubbed a hand across his chin. Three slender hairs sprouted with an itch during the last moon. After noticing them, he let everyone have a good look. Above his lip, a thin patch was taking root. Scraggly, but dark, nonetheless. His mother referring to it as a baby caterpillar infuriated him.

Despite what she thought, it wouldn't be long before Papa would have to teach him to shave.

"It's no matter, she can't stop time. I'll be an adult whether she likes it or not."

"Jacob, if I have to say it again, I'll have you pick the biggest switch you can find!" Mama's commanding tone meant business.

Times past proved his mother would keep true to her words. Man or not, he knew so long as he lived under her roof, the switch was not something she brought up unless she meant it.

"I'm coming Mama." Every other stair thudded beneath Jacob's feet.

The sight of his mother in front of the kitchen stove, tightening her apron around her petite frame, stopped Jacob in his tracks. He stood frozen, rooted to the threadbare rug in the kitchen's entryway. With one hand, she pushed back the wisps of light brown hair falling across her forehead behind her ear. With the other, her delicate fingers grasped a wooden spatula, stirring eggs in the cook pot. One would never believe she once lashed his backside so hard that even his papa had to look away. The memory was enough for him to grab at his belt loops and wiggle his breeches up, as if by doing so he could guard his bottom.

Hoping to set things right, Jacob broke the silence. "Mama, I'm sorry — I would never —"

"Jacob," said his mother, working the wooden spatula around the pan. The soft gaze of her light blue eyes did not hold the fury filling them the night before. Jacob exhaled a huge breath, unaware he held it until doing so. "Come; give your mama a hug."

Relief filled him, but he wanted to cry. Lines of worry settled across his mother's brow, and she somehow looked much older. He shoved his hands into the pockets of his trousers and lowered his eyes to the floor. *This was his fault!* The game he played kept her up the entire night fretting over him. He embraced her. "Mama, I'm sorry I played that nasty trick. Really, I am..."

"Son," she whispered, "soon enough, you'll be old enough to do things as you see fit. I can't protect you forever. But understand that Mama only tells you things for a reason. *Promise me, no matter how old you get, you won't go into those woods!*"

"I won't. I promise."

She held him an arm's length away, shaking her head. Eventually, she gave him a push toward the table. "Come now." She was already a step behind with the cook pan in hand. "You need to eat. Papa needs a lot of help today."

His mouth watered. Steaming food hit his plate and he dove into it, shoveling pieces of fried meat and eggs into his mouth.

"The nights are getting cold. Too cold. I fear the coming winter will be the worst since before you were born," his mother said, concern marking her tone.

He wiped the egg yolk clean from the plate with his last bite of bread and licked his fingers, washing it all down with milk.

"You'll need to be out there with him most days until we have enough wood and more to keep the fires lit."

"Yes, Mama." He was already on his feet, planting a kiss on her cheek before leaving to do his tasks. "You can count on me to help."

It wasn't long before he saw his father up the hill. The dull rhythm of steel beating wood told Jacob his papa was still fixing the fence. Several times the neighbors had come by, informing Papa they'd found his sheep wandering about their land.

"Fool sheep," his papa said, grumbling.

"Good morning," Jacob murmured.

His father's hair was slick with sweat, even though the sun was only peeking above the horizon. The man woke earlier than anyone he knew. Jacob once asked his friends, and they agreed their fathers waited until the sun was already up before rising from their beds. His papa grunted as he went on about his work. Steady swings of the man's hammer drove the pole into the earth.

"Mornin' lad," said the man, not looking up until the post was firm in the ground. "There's much to be done today."

Jacob nodded. Admiration filled him as he watched his father wipe the sweat from his brow. A tall man, his father was broad at the shoulders, and was easily one of the strongest men in the village. Papa was well respected by everyone. Some men even came to sit with Papa after supper, asking his counsel on matters from crops to the value of gold in various parts of the kingdom.

And for that, Jacob was proud. He wanted nothing more than to follow in his footsteps. "I'll get started on the firewood, unless you need help here..." He couldn't explain it, but he wanted nothing more than to work close to Papa today.

"Not today, boy." His father studied him.

The weight of his father's eyes made him nervous, and he shuffled his feet. "I'll help here with the fence then."

His papa shook his head, one eye squinted closed against the climbing sun. "No, son, not today..." His father scrubbed a handkerchief across the back of his neck. "Did your mama feed you?"

"Aye, she did."

"Good. I pray you learned a lesson?"

"Aye."

"You're getting a mite big for pranks and fool's games, son."

"I know."

"So long as you know, boy. There's no sense in going to bed without any supper for playing the fool."

"It wasn't worth it, Papa. Mama cooks too good a meal for me to want to miss another."

His father chuckled. Tension lifted from Jacob's shoulders.

"That's right, boy. I've missed too many myself over the years upsetting your mother. It wasn't until my belly started touching my backbone that I wisened up."

It was Jacob's turn to laugh. He could only imagine what Papa must have done to get sent to bed without supper. Jacob beamed when the man ruffled his hair.

"Today, I have one chore for you," his papa said. "And I want you to take care while you go about it."

Jacob wondered what special job his papa had for him.

"You'll make up for your prank by going to the field on the other side of the village and picking your mother the most beautiful flower you can find. Frost is coming soon, and they'll all die off until the thaw and rebirth. Take your time and look carefully. Not any old flower will do, mind you. Your mama was quite upset."

"Of course, Papa. Not any old flower will do for Mama."

"That's right, lad. Now, you're learning." His father grinned, but was quick to harden his tone. "You're not to stop and play with any of your friends, you hear? That Malachi is a bad influence. This is to be treated as any other job you'd do here with me today. I want you to think of your mother and what she's done to raise you properly. I couldn't have done it alone, and that I know."

His father's words settled upon him. Everything his mother did, she did so with love. Even her occasional harsh discipline came from the need to protect him. There was no arguing this. He couldn't ask for a better mother. And he certainly wouldn't trade her for anyone else. "I'll find the prettiest flower in the field, Papa."

"Well, you won't find it standing here all day, now will you?" His papa flashed him a smile, hammer in hand as he readied another spike-bottomed pole to beat into the earth. "Be back by midday meal."

"I wouldn't miss it," Jacob said, and set off onto the trail which led into the village of Ilrun.

THE FORBIDDEN WOOD

ILRUN

ACT II

NEATLY BUILT storefronts adorned the cobblestone walk to either side of Jacob as he made his way through pockets of people going on about their business. The aroma of fresh pastries and cakes set to cool on a windowsill at Deliran's bakery wafted upon the breeze. It was near enough to cause him to stray from his path, but he stayed the course. All around him, chatter filled the air. Snippets of conversation drifted along the breeze, and someone's words caught his attention.

"Aye, the sheep are a little thin this cycle..." One man spoke to another, his tone serious, repeating the sentiments his own parents expressed to each other in recent conversation.

This wasn't the first time Jacob heard similar concerns around the village, typically followed by villagers pondering whether or not the shortage of sheep had anything to do with the coming winter. He couldn't remember a time when people worried as much about the advancing cold. He nodded toward the men in greeting. The men returned his salutation, one tipping his hat while the other stroked his mustache quizzically.

Jacob quickened his pace upon the cobblestone street. The clanging of steel against steel rang out through the square, and a slew of cursing brought the hammering to a halt. Jacob recognized the deep, harsh voice immediately for Ral'dun McAthy. The old blacksmith tended to the horseshoes, the tools, and the few weapons in the village since his father was a boy. McAthy was hot blooded, and was as well known for his temper as much as his skill of his craft. It was said Ral'dun had taken on a new apprentice, and was none too happy with the young man's performance. His father even made mention during supper one night that old McAthy docked his apprentice a week's wages, citing the youth was jittery and didn't have an eye for the work.

"You're costing me more than your worth, boy!" McAthy's shouts floated out the open windows of the smithy. Jacob quickened his step. "You're going to cost me my smithy! And it's been in the family since before the White Rider arrived on Obsedea, when our sister world, Lilith, died!"

"I—" the apprentice started, but his protest was cut off by a loud smack.

Jacob was no more than a pace or so past the door when the apprentice cried out and came tumbling out onto the walk. "Are you alright?" Jacob asked, looking down at the man who was only a few cycles older than himself. "Let me help you up."

An angry red welt was swelling on the man's cheek. "But the work I did was perfect," said the apprentice, clearly dazed. "There weren't any flaws in the work. I made sure of it."

"Here," said Jacob, annoyance bringing heat to his cheeks. He helped the man up. "I'm sure you did a fine job, but I have to be on my way." He gave the apprentice an obligatory dusting off and wasted no time putting as much distance between himself and the smithy as he could. The last thing he needed was Old McAthy heaping more trouble onto his plate.

Shops came and went. Jacob navigated his way through the perfectly lined rows of cottages which housed those who lived and worked within the village. Though closer together and smaller, the homes were no different than where his family lived. Papa always told him he needed open space, and that he felt he couldn't breathe if he was in the village for almost any length of time. The village, his father claimed, was no place to raise a family.

Jacob's boots clunked across what remained of the cobblestone. He paused for a moment and looked over his shoulder. Melancholy wrapped him in a cold embrace. From the outskirts of the village, Ilrun appeared much smaller now than it did when he was younger.

The air was sweet and he filled his lungs, taking in the lush grasses of the open field. Morning dew clung to the emerald blades, glistening in the light of the climbing sun. The green expanse was ornamented with flowers of all colors and sizes, standing out like glinting gems across the landscape.

It was custom in Xaentis for every village to set aside a patch of land to grow and nurture a flower from each of its neighbors. It was made law in a time long past, or so his father told him. The king in those times claimed it was a sign of good will and harmony, determined it would keep all of the realm strong and united against the plots and schemes of other kingdoms.

"Jacob!" Behind him, the sound of his name interrupted his thoughts. His friend, Malachi, waved to him from the edge of the village. "What are you doing out here?"

"I could ask the same of you," said Jacob, grinning at his friend.

"Ma sent me to the market to fetch some Teri root. Isabella has gone and caught a cold. Now I'm stuck playing the errand boy."

"You're quite a way from the market. Doesn't seem to me you're too worried about her." Jacob stifled a laugh. He'd always wanted a little brother or sister, but Malachi insisted it was more trouble than it was worth. When Malachi didn't find any humor in the situation, Jacob asked, "Will she be alright?"

"She should be. She's always falling sick. If you ask me, it's all a show to keep from doing chores and pulling her weight."

"You really think so?"

"Of course, I do. She always gets sick before winter. It's when we have the most work out at our place."

"Aye, it's the same at ours, but at least you have a sister to help most of the time. Even if she does play at being sick."

Pow! Malachi's fist landed on his arm before he realized his friend even swung.

"You jack rabbit!" Jacob rubbed at his arm. *"Why would you do that?"*

"Because you're defending her, that's why."

"I'm not." Jacob clenched a fist.

"It's no secret you want to dance with her during the Rebirth Festival, next cycle. You'll both be of age. Good luck if you make her your wife. As much as she's weaseled her way out of things over the years, I don't think she knows how to cook a meal, let alone wash a dish." Malachi barked a laugh. Heat burned in Jacob's cheeks. He lunged.

They hit the ground, and Jacob wailed on the boy beneath him. *"I'm not making anyone my wife!"*

"Get off me!" Malachi pushed upwards from the ground, rolling Jacob off of him.

For some time they lay panting, as though they'd run a race from the village to Jacob's house and back. While the peace lasted, Jacob allowed himself to calm down and his eye caught a large crow slowly circling the sky above. The bird glided along the length of a cloud as it crossed the sun, little more than a silhouette against the fiery orb.

Papa always told him to be wary of crows. Devious creatures, his father insisted, conjured up by witchcraft. If one was to meet your eye, it would forever remember your face. Papa warned him misfortune was sure to follow.

Jacob snorted. For as much as he admired Papa, the man could be as big a fool as a child afraid of the dark. More than once, his father cautioned him against wolves and spooks. Papa's tales were always grim in the telling. Stories of people he'd never seen in faraway places he'd never been, all meeting their end cruelly by some evil twist of darkness.

"You're a fool, Papa," Jacob said, chuckling.

"What's that?" Malachi asked.

"Oh, nothing. I was just thinking of how my papa believes in bedtime stories."

"Like what?"

"Take that bird for example," said Jacob, pointing toward the crow which was now engaged in a leisurely descent. "Papa believes crows to be the eyes of witches in hiding. Sent out to spy on people like us."

Malachi's eyes widened. *"Do you believe it?"*

"Of course not. Do you?"

"What kind of question is that? Do I look like a babe just off the teat?"

"Only a smidgen!" Jacob laughed, and stood, extending his hand to the boy.

"Well, I still look older than you," said Malachi, a self-satisfied smirk across his lips.

Once they were both on their feet and brushed off, Malachi pressed him for further details, curious to what else Jacob's father warned him of. Jacob didn't have to think long.

"Well, aside from not lending your papa any coin," he started to say, before he caught the fiery warning in his friend's eyes. "I mean to say, he and my mother believe the same as most everyone else. That something sinister dwells in the woods."

Malachi gazed toward the tree line at the edge of the field.

"Just last night I got sent to bed without a bite to eat for having a joke with Mama." Jacob shook his head, remembering the consequences of his actions. "Told her I went in. At first, I thought she was going to die of shock right there! Then I was worried she was going to beat me."

"That's rough," said Malachi, shielding his eyes against the sun.

"Aye. It's why I'm out here now. Papa thinks it would be wise I fetch a flower for her today."

Malachi belted out a raucous laugh and slapped his knee. "I'd say it serves you right. Even grown men know better than to say as much! You're a fool."

Heat flushed his cheeks while Malachi cackled. He jabbed his finger into the chest of his friend. "And what's so funny?"

"I think it's lovely that you're out here to pick your ma a flower. *Will you nestle at her breast for your midday milk after giving it to her?*"

Jacob shoved his friend. "Why is it I'm the fool, and not Mama and Papa, for believing such a fancy? It should be them you're laughing at, not me."

Malachi shrugged. Jacob stomped off, grumbling. He scanned the nearby field of flowers before him. Examining the pink petals of a flower from Sirad, a village to the west of Ilrun, he asked, "And what of your parents? What say them?"

"My mam and pap say the same thing. I'm not to go beyond the field. Not even if my head is cut off and rolls right into the woods."

"And do they tell you why?"

"Same as everyone is told. That evil lives in there." Malachi's face twisted with uncertainty and he looked to the woods.

"I thought you didn't believe in bedtime stories?" Jacob's eyes landed on the thorny-stemmed flower of Canyth.

"It's not a bedtime story," Malachi said. "Even the eldest in Ilrun say to stay out."

"If there is something evil lurking in there, why won't anyone say what it is? If you so much as bring it up, you're likely to get a beating for your effort."

"Aye. I brought it up one night when my pap was drinking. He'd been in good spirits until then. He belted me until the sun came up."

"See what I mean? The tale has been passed on for so long that everyone just accepts it. No one questions it."

Malachi crossed his arms and shook his head. "Even if there isn't anything to be found in there, you won't catch me risking my hide to go exploring."

"You're as scared as the rest of them." Jacob kicked at the grass.

"Maybe so..." Malachi shrugged. "But even the oldest stories have some truth to them. That's what Granpap always tells me."

"Your granpap is as dumb-" There was no chance to finish when an ear-piercing shriek from above froze his blood.

"By the White Rider!" cried Malachi.

Panic rushed through Jacob. The crow he'd been observing before was no longer gliding upon the wind. *Instead, it was diving at him with the speed of falling lightning!* His heart pounded in his chest and he guarded his face with an arm. The crow screamed and a loud whoosh of air sent him stumbling back a step. He lowered his arm enough to peek above his sleeve. The crazed bird beat at him with its wing before rising high once more.

"We— we have to go!" Malachi's voice was desperate in its insistence.

Jacob couldn't agree more. "I know! My parents will never believe me. Mama will skin me, and Papa will feed me to the dogs. After what I did last night, they might not ever believe anything I say!"

"That doesn't matter now! We have to get out of here! Before it comes back!" Urgency marked Malachi's face. His eyes darted back and forth, searching the sky. "It's coming back around! *Run!*"

None of it felt real to Jacob when his friend darted off, Malachi's boots sliding in the wet grass. It was as if time decided to slow down a second or two, stretching out its pace as it marched on forever. He couldn't help but look up. When he did, he realized the bird was quickly descending upon him, close enough for him to see that the ghastly crow possessed only one eye.

The crow's eye was grotesque and bulging. In the socket where the other eye once was, an infestation of maggots churned, packing the void tight in a crawling mass. A deafening screech rang out, chilling his blood and causing his ears to ring. Off balance, he started to run.

"Malachi, help me!" Jacob screamed after his friend. To his dismay, Malachi was now at the far end of the field, dashing toward the village.

Malachi did not look back.

The crow's beak pierced Jacob's shoulder. The bird tore at him, slicing his flesh. Agony seared the length of his arm and he hit the ground. Terrified, he grappled himself up, stumbling forward.

A boot caught in a hole, and he nearly lost his footing. By the grace of the White Rider, he remained upright. A treacherous cry from the bird sent daggers of ice tearing at his insides.

"Leave me be, witch!" he cursed. It did no good, the crow continuing its vicious assault.

The creature forced Jacob to dive. Had he looked before throwing himself to the earth, perhaps he would have noticed the root. But it was too late. His mind sloshed when his head smacked the petrified wood. White stars blazed in his vision.

Why is the ground so hard? The thought was faint. *The ground is hard, and I need to get mama a flower.*

Jacob opened his eyes and willed himself to focus. A root as thick as a man's arm protruded from the earth, leading into a dark, decay-riddled tree which towered above him. The tree was sickly, its limbs leafless and rotting. Its branches went every which way, entangled with one another, creating an impenetrable web. "The edge of the field. I shouldn't be here."

He made to stand, but his entire body trembled with the effort it took to make it to his knees. Jacob did the best he could to sort his wits.

"I must have knocked my head on that dratted root." His throat felt raw. He'd like nothing more than to be sitting a spell with his papa, having a cool cup of his mother's lemon water.

He smiled at the thought, but his attention was ripped away when the crow shrieked from above. Plagued with fear, it drove him to his feet and propelled him forward, darting past the menacing tree.

ACT III

DARKNESS ENVELOPED Jacob as the sun vanished above the thick canopy of branches. He dared not move, and closed his eyes, allowing them a moment to adjust. When he opened them again, he could barely see. A chill tiptoed up his spine, a chicken thief creeping into the henhouse, hoping to not get caught. No matter where he looked there were trees, all of which were splattered with mold and blotches of crusted grey that oozed sappy liquid like infected, picked scabs. None of the trees stood tall and proud like those around his home. Instead, they resembled bent over old men who'd worked a day too many during their long lives.

Jacob's belly turned when the smell of death wafted past his nose. "Aaak!" He dry heaved. "Yuck."

He spat, noticing the floor of the woods was nothing more than dark earth littered with fungi and dead trees which no longer stood among their brethren.

A step forward caused a loud crack as a branch snapped beneath his feet. This time he did vomit, the noise pushing his nerves beyond their limit. For several moments, all he could do was empty his stomach in a steaming hurl until there was nothing left. *This is wrong. I need to get out of here. I need to go home and tell Mama and Papa everything.*

What he saw next was more than he could bear. *No. This isn't real. It can't be.*

The line of trees separating him from the field was much thicker than before. It was as though the rotting growth had multiplied, creating a wall he would not be able to pass through. And if this was not enough, atop every branch perched a crow, each as dark as night and missing the same eye as the one who'd chased him here.

Disbelief gnawed at him. He even went so far as to pinch his arm in an attempt to wake himself. The pain did nothing save leave a nasty red mark on his flesh. Never before in all his life could he remember feeling this helpless. His vision blurred with fresh tears. A string of mucus leaked from his nose and clung to his lip.

"Go! Just go and leave me alone!" he shouted.

Caw! The crows' cries pierced his soul. The birds cocked their heads in unison, studying Jacob like predators stalking prey, formulating the best method of attack. If there was anything left in his stomach, he was sure he'd have retched again. He shuffled a step backward. Horror stuck in his throat when the trees moved with him, closing any space left between their branches.

I swear on my life. If this ends, I'll never pull another fool prank again. The thought was gone as quickly as it came. It didn't take him long to realize his options were limited. There was no hope in escaping the same way he'd come.

"I can only go the other way and pray the White Rider will guide me out. *But what if I can't get out?*" He wiped his eyes and the crows blinked at him as if the murder was of one mind. He made his decision.

The earth shifted beneath him when he ground a heel into the soil. He pivoted hard and his back was to the crows. A quick breath of the stale, stinking air was all the time he allowed himself. He burst forward.

A thousand wings beat at the air in fury. Jacob dared a look back long enough to see the birds taking flight. *Maybe they've had enough.* The hope was extinguished when a dozen or so of the foul creatures began circling around him.

"Get away from me!" He swung an arm. His fist connected with one of the crows in a sickening crunch. Delight danced in his belly. The victory was short lived when beaks as sharp as his mother's cooking knives began to slash at him from all sides.

For what seemed like an eternity, Jacob endured the relentless attack. Little more than scarlet tatters, his shirt was warm with blood. Each step was an excruciating task. He was convinced that at any moment he would fall over dead. *I can't take much more of this. I'm going to die here. I love you, Mama. And you too, Papa. I'm so sorry.*

He tumbled to the earth. He couldn't brace himself against the fall. The soil was soft and cool against the heat steaming from his body. Goose pimples sprang up his entire length. Whether or not the crows still assaulted him, he did not know. His flesh was numb. All in all, it didn't matter if they picked his bones clean. No one would venture into the woods to find him.

Time ceased to exist, as did everything else around him. The only thing touching his awareness was his own beating heart. And even so, just faintly. Images of his mother swam through his mind. Whether preparing his favorite meal, or sharing the rare, inappropriate joke with him, the happiest times he'd spent with her played out before him as if he were living them all over again.

While the scenes unfolded, his mother became younger until eventually she looked to be only a bit older than he was now. He couldn't recall having ever seen her this way. So young and pretty. Joy flooded him when she leaned in to plant a kiss on his forehead and began to sing to him a lullaby he fondly remembered.

> *"Away from the woods*
> *Boy,*
> *Promise you'll stay*
> *Take heed,*
> *I do pray son,*
> *The words*
> *That I say.*
>
> *For veiled in the wood*
> *An evil does live,*
> *Disguised behind lies*
> *And beautiful gifts.*
>
> *Away from the woods,*
> *Boy,*
> *Promise this day,*
> *Away from the woods,*
> *Boy,*
> *Promise you'll stay.*
>
> *So listen my son,*
> *Take heed and obey.*
> *Away from the woods son,*
> *Is what your mother does say."*

Jacob didn't know for how long she sang to him, nor did he care, enjoying the blissful moment and his mother's love. As far as he was concerned, this could go on without end, but was dismayed when the singing stopped and she vanished, his name echoing as she disappeared. *"Jacob..."*

A grunt of pain escaped him, and he blinked open his eyes. "Mama?" he asked. He pushed himself up. "Is that you?"

"Jacob, come to me..." The voice was distant, and he lurched toward it.

"Where are you?" he croaked, his eyes scanning the terrain.

Searching the space that surrounded him, he couldn't help but notice that the crows were no longer present. *Surely, I've caught a fever, and am delusional in bed. I'll wake any moment, and that's that. Wake up! Wake up! Wake up!*

His heart skipped a beat when the voice continued on, echoing the words of the lullaby his mother so lovingly sang to him.

It has to be Mama. he thought. The earth was soft against his elbows when he pushed himself upward. *She's the only one who knows that song. She said it's her song just for me.*

He abandoned caution and made in the direction from whence the singing came. He moved no more than a step when he jerked to a halt. His flesh cried out in suffering from the fiery lacerations inflicted by the abhorrent crows. Carefully, he limped along.

Eventually he found himself in a clearing and rested his gaze upon a dozen or so towering stones which stood as tall as the trees. The stones were smooth, appearing to have been weather beaten for countless cycles. Half circle, the stones were set into the shape of a crescent moon. "Mama?" He scanned the area, the song so loud he almost wanted to cover his ears. "I can hear you. *Please, I'm here!*"

Jacob's heart was racing, and he held his breath. When the lullaby came to an abrupt silence, he swept his eyes back and forth, seeking her in the spaces between the stones. Jacob's desperate search yielded no clues as to where she might be. "Mama? I can't find you. Why did you stop singing?"

To his dismay, his callings went unanswered. Knots twisted in his belly. Doubt crept along the edges of his mind. *Was the lullaby a figment of his imagination? Another turn in the nightmare he found impossible to escape?*

Despair engulfed him. There was nothing here. If he was to survive, he'd have to move on. With a sigh, he was about to set off when a voice questioned him.

"Is someone there?"

"I thought I imagined you—" he started, but lost his breath when the most beautiful woman he'd ever laid eyes on stepped out from behind a tall stone at the center of the crescent.

"You did not imagine me," said the woman. Her rosebud lips lifted in an enchanting smile. "I'm here, same as you."

*"Wh—who are y—*you?" Jacob's words tripped over his tongue and past his lips.

He surmised she was three or four cycles older than himself. The woman's attire highlighted her graceful silhouette. A violet dress hugged her shape, revealing ample curves. Draped around her neck, she wore a gemstone necklace of reds and blues, the likes of which he'd never seen before on any woman in Ilrun. Her hair hung to her shoulders in raven ringlets, bouncing ever so slightly as she approached him.

"I'm the one who lives here, of course." Her smile broadened and she shrugged.

For the first time since entering this dreadful place, Jacob relaxed. He returned her smile. "I'm Jacob."

"A pleasure, Jacob," she said. She took a step towards him and leaned in, inspecting him at closer range. Her dark, cat-like eyes sparkled with tiny flecks of gold that danced within them like flames. Momentarily mesmerized, he stood without moving while her flickering orbs took in the disheveled sight of him. "You seem to be scraped up good from the brush and the trees."

"If only it was that," he said. Worry crept over him as he examined the gashes on his arms, furiously red and caked in dirt. "But it was a cursed crow. Chased me in from the field. Then his whole family and their friends seemed to appear from nowhere and let me have it!"

"You poor dear!" The young woman gasped, reaching out to him.

He flinched when she touched him, but all his worry melted as warmth filled him the moment after her fingers made contact with his skin. "What are you doing?"

"Shh. Be still. I'm almost done." A white glow surrounded them in an illustrious bubble and faded away not even a moment after appearing. "There, that should do it. How do you feel?"

But how? Unable to formulate a response, Jacob's mouth dropped open. All of his pain ceased to exist. His skin was as clean as if he'd soaked in a hot bath. Every mark and abrasion that had been there moments before was now gone, the flesh healed, pink and smooth. Besides that, his clothes appeared mended and laundered, showing no trace of the horrific assault.

"I f—feel like n—new," he stammered in disbelief. He wiggled his fingers in front of his eyes before glancing at her. *"How did you do that?"*

She chuckled and cupped his chin, her gaze penetrating, piercing him deep beyond his eyes. Jacob could not help but be captivated by her stare. Even if he tried, he could not look away. Nor did he want to. *Is this what it felt like to fall in love?*

"I can do many things." The woman smiled, eyes twinkling brighter than a star filled sky on a summer night. *"I can even do things far greater than this."*

"How could anything be greater than this?" he asked. *Surely, he must look like a simpleton in her eyes.* "Do you think you could do away with that nasty old crow and his pals?"

She arched an eyebrow, but said nothing. An uncomfortable silence settled in between them. He worked his brow and attempted to puzzle out what he'd said to earn such a quizzical eye. If this wasn't nerve wracking enough, the wretched bird appeared suddenly and sat upon her shoulder. Fear plunged him into its icy depths when he noticed how comfortable the creature was, as though it was perched upon its favorite branch.

The crow cocked its head, seeming to mock him. A maggot, twice the size of any of the others, fell from where there had once been a second eye and landed on its beak. The bird opened its beak, inviting the maggot to wiggle its way into the crevice before snapping shut and swallowing the morsel down.

"Why would I do away with Victor? He's been a loyal pet to me for as long as I can remember." She patted the bird gently on its beak as if she was its mother tapping its nose.

"He tried to kill me!" It was hard to command his emotions. "You saw what your—*your Victor* did to me."

"He was only protecting me."

"He drove me into these woods!" *Did she not know what a dangerous creature her precious pet was?* Jacob couldn't believe his eyes when the woman shook her head at him. She made him feel as if he was a foolish child with the inability to understand.

"Are you not healed of any pain he may have caused you?"

"I am, but that's not the—"

"If you are healed, then why are you going on, crying like a child? Why, I thought you were a man, given the mustache and beard you wear."

She grinned at him. Before he knew it, she was stroking the whiskers on his chin.

"As a matter of fact, I wasn't crying." Jacob was taken aback by her statement and wanted nothing more in that moment than to look a man in her eyes. It was the first time anyone paid him a compliment to his mustache. At home, he was lucky if his mama and papa even snickered when he brought it up.

"I didn't think so." She smiled once more, and the curve of her perfect rosebud lips became the focus of his attention. The crow perched menacingly on her shoulder faded into the background. "Come, you must be hungry. I'm sure you haven't enjoyed a midday meal yet, being out here in these woods."

"That would be wonderful, and I am hungry. But I really need to be on my way," said Jacob. Despite his words, he followed.

She chuckled as she led him beyond the crescent-moon structure and down into a ravine where a splendid house of stones sat snuggled into the basin. Heat flushed his cheeks when he realized he'd been following the sway of her hips, eyes going from side to side as her bottom moved in time to her step.

"Really, you don't understand... If you could just tell Victor to allow me passage safely back to the field—" he began, but was awestruck into silence when she opened the door to her dwelling.

A lavish sitting room adorned with a sofa and several chairs offered anyone who might be weary a chance to get off their feet. A few paces off from the main room was a sizable table intricately carved of heavy oak, with space enough for six people to sup comfortably. Beyond that was a smaller room hosting a desk littered with parchments and scrolls. A warm fire coming from the hearth blanketed the space in an orange glow, several burning logs radiating a comforting heat.

"Welcome to my home," she said, an element of pure joy rich in her words. The sweet, welcoming sound of her melodic voice overwhelmed him with a sense of something unfamiliar, a feeling no girl from the village had ever conjured up within him before. Not even Isabella caused his heart to thump so.

"It's not much, but it's quiet, and away from Ilrun. I don't think I could ever live in the village. I feel like I can't breathe there. I've always said, if I ever wanted to raise a family, the village was no place to do so."

Jacob grinned. "Papa says the same thing all the time."

"I think I need to meet your father." She flashed him a wink.

"Papa wouldn't step foot in the woods for a whole bag full of coin!"

The two of them shared a laugh. At last the laugh petered out, and the woman spoke. "Where are my manners? Allow me to get you some tea and cakes. Please have a seat." She gestured toward the table and scurried off to a cook stove in the corner.

Jacob sat comfortably. He thought of how cozy it would be to have a place like this out here when he was finally ready to leave his parents' home. How silly that his entire life he'd been led to believe some evil lurked in these woods! On the contrary, the young woman was harmless. More so, *she was kind, gracious–the most lovely being he was blessed to have ever encountered before*. If he was careful in the way he played his hand, he could charm her into saving herself for him until the day he reached his fourteenth cycle.

"Here we are," she said, setting a steaming cup of tea down before him.

"Thank you!" In his mind, he followed those words by kissing her soft, perfect lips.

"You are most welcome. Oh, and before I forget—" She hurried to the stove and was quick to return carrying a plate filled with cinnamon cakes. "These are fresh out of the oven."

"*Cinnamon cakes?*" Jacob's mouth watered at the sight of them. "These are my favorite!"

"I suspected as much." She caressed his cheek with a finger and seated herself beside him.

"But how could you possibly know?"

"Call it intuition," she said, and giggled.

"Whatever you call it, these are brilliant!" He tried his best to not shovel the cakes into his mouth, yet failed miserably.

Ravished by hunger, the cakes were soon gone. What crumbs remained he picked up with his fingers and licked them clean.

"I'm glad you enjoyed them," she crooned and was off with his plate before he even knew she stood up. "Be sure to drink your tea before it gets cold."

Obedient to her request, Jacob raised the cup to his lips. Gently, he blew on the steaming brew and took a sip. The elixir tasted of honey and spring pepper. As it traveled down his throat, it sent a wave of butterflies fluttering through his belly. Sweat prickled upon his brow. The hair on his arms stiffened and, for a moment, his vision blurred. He struggled to focus. *Why couldn't he see straight?* The entire room vibrated and the walls crept closer, closing in on him. Everything began to spiral endlessly into clusters which resembled the inner workings of a bee's hive.

"What's going on?" Jacob asked, and gasped. Panic traced his mind, a delicate finger outlining his deepest fears and shedding light upon them.

"What do you mean?" The woman's voice was far away.

Words were lost to him as the knots of hexagonal prisms claimed the entirety of the room and continued to flow forward into his line of vision. His knuckles cracked as he clutched the sides of his seat. Objects and colors no longer made any sense at all. Shockwaves of light reverberated in his mind. A cataclysmic thunderous crash echoed through him, the destruction colliding into the core of his being. *I am no longer Jacob of Ilrun,* he thought. *I am the world Lilith, dying all over again!*

A scream clawed its way up Jacob's throat and he felt incapacitated, wanting nothing more than to let it escape, but it was helplessly barred behind the cage of his teeth. *Everything was wrong here. He needed to go home. By the White Rider, he needed to go home, right now!*

Jacob squeezed his eyes shut and silently screamed these words in his mind. The moment he did, the nightmare came to a screeching halt. The storm within vanished and all was calm. The hexagonal prison entrapping him evaporated, his vision restored.

He released his grip on the chair. Relief soared through his aching hands. Any knot, pain, or discomfort he could ever remember was gone, and he felt as if he was nothing more than the rippling waters in a washtub.

His muscles released every bit of tension they held moments before and he could no longer be bothered to keep his body in an upright sitting position. He was aware of his body sliding downward, from the chair to the floor, but couldn't be bothered to stop. A permanent grin parted his lips, and all he could do was laugh. Everything was beautiful.

"What are you doing on the floor?" asked the woman.

Jacob only laughed and pounded his fists on the floor. "I haven't the slightest clue, but it feels amazing!"

"Get up, you silly man."

Her use of the word man caused excitement to swell in his trousers and nearly played a hand in pushing himself up.

Hot tears rolled down his cheeks, and he started to cough. Whatever the reason, this too was funny, and he doubled over, his stomach wrenching in protest. What a delightful feeling this was! Surely, the most wonderful feeling he'd experienced in all of his life! Incomparable, even, to the time he and Malachi snuck into Dalando Thatcher's wine cellar and stole a bottle of the man's stock last summer.

"Come, let's get you to the sofa," said the woman.

Jacob did not object, following behind her as she led the way. She took a seat first, then ran her fingertips across the couch's velvet cushion; an invitation for Jacob to join her. Fascinated by her every move, his eyes did not leave her fingertips when, without hesitation, he sank into the seat next to her. Enraptured by her enchanting beauty, Jacob's eyes lifted from her fingertips, traced the outline of her curves, and lingered on her lips, before meeting her line of vision.

Her exotic eyes, reflecting pools of liquid fire, mesmerized him. Whether he wanted to drown within them or burn forever in their dancing flames, Jacob did not know... nor did it matter. When she smiled, the flames within grew brighter. She blushed, but did not turn away. Seeing her vulnerability, he wished to know the feel of her lips on his. In this moment, Jacob's inexperience mattered not. He felt himself the man he wanted others to see him as, because this was the way she looked at him.

He pushed away intrusive thoughts of returning home, of Mama's flower, of things previously important. He would stay as long as the woman would allow him to. *He would not leave until stealing that kiss!* Returning home late would be well worth any punishment his parents bestowed upon him, including the kind where Mama forced him to go outside to find his own switch, before whopping him senseless. Even better, Malachi would surely turn green with envy once he learned what he missed out on, running back to the village without a second thought, and leaving Jacob to fend for himself.

"I've never felt so good!" Confidence coursed through him. He reached out to touch her.

"That makes me happy." She batted her eyelashes. She didn't stop him when his fingers brushed across the silk of her cheek.

"You never did tell me your name." He smirked but she pressed a finger to his lips.

"I told you, I'm the one who lives here."

"But—"

"I want to know about you, Jacob. *Everything.*"

ACT IV

TIME CEASED to exist and Jacob animated in the telling of his tales of life in Ilrun. Everything he could remember about himself, his mama and papa, even the times he'd gotten into trouble with Malachi, he shared with enthusiasm down to the tiniest of details. His heart skipped a beat when the woman rested her hands on his knee, eyes sparkling as she hung on to his every word.

"Malachi was so angry I beat him in the foot race! He wouldn't even talk to me for a week!" he boasted. "He even told his papa I cheated. And my papa doesn't trust Malachi's papa. Papa says he once borrowed some coin from him and he still hasn't paid him back. He even said the fellow will walk around the entire village just to avoid him if he sees Papa coming his way. *Can you believe it?*"

She shook her head and for a moment there was silence. It pained his heart his mother wasn't here to enjoy such a time, to see there was nothing to be afraid of in these woods. Despite his earlier misgivings, he could even forgive Victor's assault on him. Surely, if the crow was only protecting the woman, who was he to hold a grudge?

"What are you thinking about?" the woman asked.

"Oh nothing. It's silly," he said. The last thing he wanted was to ruin the moment with talk of his mother. Especially when the most beautiful woman he'd ever laid eyes on was sitting only a breath away.

"Very well, then." She made to stand.

"Wait." He took her hand in his. "I was thinking about my mama. She's a sweet woman. The sweetest I know, truth be told. Please don't get me wrong, I love her. But I pity her too. A woman her age believing in bedtime tales and ghouls. Why, if not for Victor, you and I would have never met. I'm not allowed to be here. I was sent to bed with no supper last night just for saying I'd been."

"Such a shame." The woman squeezed his hand and her eyes were solemn. "All too often people have the wrong ideas about how this world works."

He inclined his head and cleared his throat. "How did you heal me?"

"I told you, I can do even greater things than that."

He studied her, looking for any tell he could find. "What else can you do?"

She hesitated, but he insisted. "Come on now. You know everything about me. It's your turn. Can you kiss a frog and turn him into a prince?"

The woman only looked away when he chuckled. A brief silence passed, nearly suffocating Jacob, until the woman cleared her throat. "Nothing. It's—It's silly."

The woman's cheeks burned scarlet, and her eyes darted to the floor. *She was nervous!*

Jacob gaped in disbelief, but was quick to respond. "Oh no, you don't! That line didn't work for me. It won't work for you."

"Do you promise you won't laugh at me?" She met his eyes once more.

"I swear on the White Rider."

The woman seemed to cringe at his words, but smoothed her features. "Very well, I'll tell you. But only because you promised not to laugh. *I can grant you one wish. Any wish you want."*

Jacob kept his promise. He didn't laugh. There was nothing funny about it. The idea was ridiculous. Was everyone like this? Superstitious and conjuring up fool fantasies of witches and wishes? He wouldn't say any of this to her, of course, though he couldn't help but sigh.

Yet, his mind was intent on playing back images of their initial meeting. He recalled the way it felt when she first placed her hands upon his skin. He held his arms in front of him, searching for any sign of Victor's attack. He could not find a single scratch. Jacob chastised himself for doubting her words. *She did heal you back there, fool. Think about it. Not a mark on you from the crow. How do you explain that?*

"Would you like me to prove it to you? What do you have to lose?" Her lips twitched into a smile. "If I can do as I say, you get whatever you wish for. If I can't, then we both have a good laugh anyway."

He considered her offer for some time. *What if she is testing me? What if this is some kind of trick to measure whether or not I believe in such childish things?*

The woman tapped her slippered foot upon the floor. "Tell me, Jacob, what will it be?"

"Ok then, show me."

"Very well." She grinned.

The room spun into darkness. Ice burrowed into his bones, the warmth and the light from the fire gone from existence.

"Wh – what's happening?" The question trembled from his lips." Why is it so dark? *I can't see anything!*"

His legs grew weak beneath him. He reached out into the darkness, searching for the woman, only to grab fistfuls of air in return. His mind felt heavy, and he was confused. *"Help me! Someone!"* His knees buckled, and he collapsed, slipping into an uncomfortable sleep.

The scratching of what sounded to be a lucifer against stone woke him. The fire starter ignited with a luminous *snap*, and cast a dim light in the space surrounding him. It took a moment for his eyes to adjust. When they did, he followed the flame of the lucifer until a twin flame was born in the darkness. As the light chased away shadow, he could make out the second source to be a flame burning atop what looked to be a tall candle.

"It's quite alright, Jacob." The woman's voice was faint. The flame flickered and came toward him. *"Are you hurt?"*

"I'm not sure, but I don't think so–" He started to speak, but cut his words short when he tried to move, and couldn't.

Steel cracked against stone when he jerked his arm, and his wrist felt as if it was in the grasp of an iron-clawed giant. The motion of the effort sent the arm swinging back, and he yelped in agony when his elbow crashed into the unforgiving surface behind him.

"What's going on here?" Jacob's question was met with laughter, coming out of the darkness from either side of him. Terror choked him. He was able to move his head only enough to realize he was chained naked to a wall. Icy fingers of fear wrapped around his heart. His eyes darted around the room. By the looks of things, he appeared to be in some sort of cellar. The floor was frigid against his feet and made up of packed dirt. *"Where are we?"*

The flame atop the candle danced and blinked, coming closer when a deep voice he did not recognize answered, "Are you so stupid? We're in a silly bedtime story. That's where we are. A silly bedtime story used to frighten children. You know the kind. It's all I've heard you go on about. A silly, stupid, bedtime story used to frighten children like *you!*"

Air rushed from Jacob's lungs when the flame grew larger, revealing a man two times the size of any he'd ever seen. Hard muscles roped the man's limbs, leading into a shirtless chest tattooed in calloused scars.

"Who are you?" Jacob asked with extreme effort, fear gripping hold of his tongue, digging its invisible claws into the soft pink flesh.

"Don't tell me you don't recognize me?" The question spat in his face stank, smelling akin to a full chamber pot left out deliberately to cook in the sun.

His mind scrambled. *Who could this monstrosity of a man be?* He'd never laid eyes on this menacing creature before, not even once in his worst nightmares. Certainly, if he had, he would remember the man's breath, if nothing else.

"Oh, c'mon, I thought we were old pals, you and me?" The man was only inches from Jacob, his every word emitting a vile stench. The glow of the candle light shone upon the man's face, a spotlight illuminating his only eye. Where the other eye should have been churned maggots the size of a child's finger, oozing out of the socket in droves and crawling into a beard made up of swarming flies.

"Victor?" Jacob flinched against the jagged stone behind him. The man's one-eyed stare bore down upon him.

"In the flesh." Victor grinned. The man's mouth resembled the beak of a bird, protruding out at a curve and coming to a razor-sharp point.

Jacob tried to bury himself into the wall of stone. The man's smile widened. His blackened tongue slithered from the beak of his mouth toward Jacob. It crawled along Jacob's cheek before slithering onto his mouth and caressing his lips. Jacob squeezed his eyes shut and tried to turn away. His stomach boiled from the awful taste of vinegar and rotting flesh. Victor's tongue peeled apart his lips, then scraped against Jacob's clenched teeth.

Jacob screamed, the sound ripped out of existence when Victor's tongue plunged down his throat and into the bottom of his belly. The legs of countless maggots raked his skin while the man pressed his face against his own.

Victor's good eye rubbed against his for what seemed an eternity before slicing pain tore at Jacob's insides, and the tongue slithered its way back out of him. Jacob struggled to breathe, his head slumping as far back as the restraints around his neck allowed.

Hoping against hope that this was some cruel punishment bestowed upon him for his prank, Jacob tried to convince himself it wasn't real. *"This isn't happening. It can't be!"*

"Oh, but it is," said the man, a vile laugh pouring from his depths.

Jacob's teeth sliced into his tongue when his head was jerked up, and his eyes were forced open by calloused fingers he could feel but couldn't see. A warm, coppery taste filled his mouth.

"Mama, Papa? Help me!" Every word was excruciating, the tip of his tongue feeling as if it was hanging on by a thread. *"Somebody wake me up!"*

"This isn't a dream, Jacob." A glimmer of hope filled him when he recognized the voice of the young woman. "This is as real as you and I."

"Help!"

The woman stepped out of the shadows and stood next to Victor.

Warmth trickled from Jacob's mouth when he spoke. *"I believe you. But I don't want a wish. Let's go back to your house."*

"But you didn't believe me, Jacob. You wanted me to prove it, remember?"

He could only groan in defeat.

"After I invited you into my home, and showed you kindness." The woman shook her head at him, disgusted. "I even healed you, but that was not enough for you to trust in me. For shame, Jacob! Perhaps your mother should have taught you some manners along with everything else. What would she say right now if she was to see you like this?"

Sweat was slick on his flesh when he remembered his nakedness. At this point, he didn't care if his mother saw him like this. *Not so long as it would end, and he could wake up.*

"She asked you a question, boy!" Victor's lashing voice cut through his thoughts. He trembled when he noticed the one-eyed man was pulling a long-bladed knife from a sheath belted on his hip.

"I—I don't know." Jacob tried carefully to speak, his injured tongue feeling as though it would tumble out of his mouth at any moment.

"That's not a very good answer, *now is it?*" Victor demanded, lunging toward him, slashing at his chest with the blade. The cold steel bit through Jacob's skin, the edge of the knife jagged and merciless as it tore him open.

"Come Jacob." The young woman's voice was frigid. "It's time. Let us find out if it's a fool or fancy. What do you wish for?"

Jacob winced when the candlelight flashed, filling the room with blinding light. As the blazing brightness dissipated, the woman flickered and swirled into thin tendrils of mist. She winked in and out of existence a dozen times, cycling before him, coming closer with each blink until she was once more flesh and bone.

The woman stood before him, same as before, yet somehow different. Jacob couldn't help but notice how dangerously beautiful she still was. She was clad in the same form-fitting dress, revealing every detail of her curves. Her breasts were as pale as moonlight, her cleavage spilling over the fabric. Eyes as yellow as the sun stared back at him, the menacing glow of her irises dancing like wildfires around pitch black pupils that morphed and lengthened, tilting at a slant. The woman's smile was wide, her lips no longer soft and inviting, but cut with gashes and torn apart. Thin, sinewy threads hung from the corners of her mouth, as though her lips had once been sewn shut, only to have the stitching later ripped away.

"What's the matter Jacob?" she asked. "Cat got your tongue?"

"*Mama!*" Jacob screamed.

The woman placed the dry, rough skin of her lips against Jacob's ear, and whispered, "If you want to suckle her breasts so bad boy, why not wish her here then?"

Panicked, Jacob closed his eyes. "*I wish my mother was here.*"

ACT V

JACOB WOKE with a start. His heart was pounding in his chest so hard he thought it would burst through his ribs. He shielded his eyes against the morning sun pouring in through the open window. He scanned the room, daring to move only when he was sure Victor and the woman were not there. The smell of damp stone was thick in his nostrils but was fading quickly. The aroma of his mother's cooking wafted its way up from the kitchen. He gave himself a quick look over, inspecting for any wounds or bleeding. Once assured he hadn't been cut and sliced, he grabbed his tongue and relief washed over him when he found it in one piece.

"Thanks be to the White Rider!" He exhaled and made for the door.

He didn't care that he wasn't wearing anything but his under bottoms as he bounded down the stairs and skidded across the kitchen floor. Happiness coursed through him when everything appeared to be in order.

I must have been dreaming the whole time. Which means I'm still in hot water with Mama. Though he was concerned, the thought wasn't enough to shake the terror still tight in his throat. *At least I'm home safe. I'll take any punishment she has for me twice.*

He gazed upon his mother, thinking about what he might say. He would do something nice for her today. He wouldn't go to the field and pick a flower. Not after what he just endured in the nightmare, but he would do something. He began thinking about how much coin he had saved to buy her a gift when she spoke, something not quite right in her voice.

"Jacob, how many times do I need to tell you to stay out of the woods?

"But Mama, I told you last night. I was only fooling. It was a joke."

"Then why did Malachi show up here red in the face saying he watched you run into the woods?"

"That was only a dream," he started, but stopped when he realized his mother wouldn't know that.

"Only a dream," she mused, setting the wooden spatula down on the cookstove.

For the first time Jacob noticed her hair was not sleek and straight. Fear trembled across his flesh.

"I'm afraid there's no hope for you. I thought perhaps one day you would be a man and listen to me," she said and turned to face him just as a screeching crow landed on her shoulder. "But apparently, you're still a stubborn child."

...TO BE CONTINUED IN BOOK II

ABOUT THE AUTHOR

RYAN ENJOYS writing everything from short stories to poetry to songs. He got his start in 2006 as a journalist for *The Courier Leader* while still in high school and later for the *Tri-City Record*. Originally from Michigan, he currently resides in Pittsburgh, PA and is working on his next novel, *Passengers*, Book 2 in the Tales of Obsedea series.

You can find more of his work as @azrael.writer on TikTok or Instagram.

Passengers: Book II Tales of Obsedea

THE AROMA of lamb stew filled the small cottage, and Virak Jagoor took a long pull from his pipe. As was tradition every Sunday, his wife was preparing a fine meal. It wouldn't be long until Atreus arrived to sup with them.

Virak sighed, exhaling a stream of blue smoke. "If only it could be a pleasant supper tonight. But I fear those days are behind us." He tapped out his pipe on the heel of a boot when his wife called for him from the kitchen.

"Virak, come help me set the table. Atreus will be here any time."

"Aye love. Here I come." Virak stood, stretching out a yawn before making his way to the kitchen.

When he arrived, Delphi was just pulling the clay dishware from a cupboard. She smiled at him. "Don't look so glum, Virak. We're not attending a funeral. We can put our worries aside long enough to enjoy supper with our son."

"Can we Delphi? Can we just sup and pretend I didn't curse my boy? My only son? We must tell him everything tonight."

Delphi sighed and set the dishware down. "I wish it didn't have to be on a Sunday. Why can't it wait until another time?"

"I told you why already. Something feels off. I've noticed strangers lurking about in Prenin. Every time I go out to do business, it seems I see one of the fellows or the other. Mark my words, wife, I know they're watching me."

"I hope it's only your nerves, but I won't say you're paranoid. I know the danger as well as you. I knew it the day you asked me to marry you."

Virak took a seat at the supper table and rested his head in his hands. "I just wish there was another one who could carry the burden."

"Me too—" Delphi started, but stopped short when the sound of the front door opening interrupted her.

"Seems Atreus is early. That's unusual for him," said Virak. He then called out, "come on boy, we're in the supping room. You're just in time."

Heavy footfalls thudded in the other room. Virak cocked his head. Atreus never stomped through the house like that. As a matter of fact, the lad was always good about taking his boots off at the door so as to keep his mother from getting upset over a dirty floor.

Virak stood, casting an eye to Delphi. He called out once more, "Atreus, you're early. What's the occasion?"

Concern flooded him when there was no response. Yet the footfalls came closer. He glanced at his wife again, but she only shrugged. It wasn't like Atreus to not respond when called. Virak started toward the sitting room to meet the boy. He'd no more than rounded the corner when a man bigger than any he'd ever seen stepped into the narrow hall.

"Who are you?" Virak demanded. He took a stance, filling the gap between the monster of a man and his wife. The man said nothing. Virak backed closer to Delphi. "You get out of my home! Right now! You have no right letting yourself in here!"

The man stepped closer. The thudding of his boots sent icy fingers prickling down Virak's spine. He pressed against his wife further, and a sickening fear churned in his stomach. He and Delphi were now backed against the wall and the intruder stopped. Virak held his breath.

Before he could understand what was happening, the brute smiled and evaporated into a wispy cloud, spinning into a whirlwind of black smoke and feathers.

And a crow screamed...

Printed in the USA
CPSIA information can be obtained
at www.ICGtesting.com
CBHW031124230724
12031CB00028B/150

9 798768 181376